Don't Go There

Arla Jones

Copyright © 2023 by Arla Jones

All rights reserved.

No part of this publication may be reproduced, distributed, or transmitted in any form or by any means, including photocopying, recording, or other electronic or mechanical methods, without the prior written permission of the publisher, except as permitted by U.S. copyright law. For permission requests, contact authorarlajones at gmail.com.

The story, all names, characters, and incidents portrayed in this production are fictitious. No identification with actual persons (living or deceased), places, buildings, and products is intended or should be inferred.

Book Cover by Dom Sabasti

Edited by Kate Seger

The Scene break image by TMT Cover Design

AI has been used to create the cover and interior images (Midjourney)

1st edition 2023

This has also been published on Vella.

Acknowledgements

I would like to thank my editor Kate Seger, TMT Cover Design for the scene break image, and also my cover artist Dom Sabasti.

Contents

Fullpage image	1
1. Let's Go!	2
2. The accident	6
3. Where to Go?	10
4. The Village	15
5. The Inn	19
6. The First Night	24
7. The Ghostly Creatures	29
8. The Ghosts Appear	35
9. The Ghosts Return to the Water	40
10. The Rest of the Night	45
11. At Breakfast	50
12. The story behind the ghosts	56

13.	The Decision to Stay in the Village	60
14.	The Ghost Village during Daylight	65
15.	The Ghost Cat and the Village	72
16.	Back in the Ship	77
17.	The Time Loop	81
18.	Walter's Story	87
19.	How to Stop the Ghosts	92
20.	The Ghosts return	97
21.	The Epilogue	104
About the author		111
Also by author Arla Jones		112

Chapter 1

Let's Go!

"Hurry! I want to get at least to Buffalo tonight. I packed some snacks, and we can buy more on the way." Sara twirled around smiling, and her happiness was contagious. Her long blond hair shone in the sunshine that filtered through the open doorway to their small single-family house.

"I'm ready whenever you are." Granger grinned as he looked at her new bride. They had decided to take a road trip for their honeymoon instead of reserving a hotel room in an exotic location. He was a tall, muscular man, the kind you'd see in the Baywatch movie, with golden tan skin and a contagious smile.

He closed the door after Sara danced from the front steps down to the driveway toward their car.

Their twenty-year-old, maroon-colored minivan was packed with their luggage, fishing poles, and two cameras, as Sara was a keen photographer. She wanted plenty of pictures to choose from for her new project, including images of America in different cities and villages, not fancy postcard pictures, but real people with wrinkles, stooped backs, homeless people, stray dogs, and cats. That was one of the reasons they planned to use their honeymoon to advance her career and get her plenty of material for the project.

Granger was a football coach at a local college, and he had taken some time off from work. Everyone understood that the newlyweds wanted to spend time together.

Granger opened the passenger side door to Sara, and she gave him a quick kiss before settling down on her seat. She had a small compact camera in her lap to take pictures while they drove.

Granger opened the driver's side door and sat down. "Did we forget anything?"

"No, I don't think so. We have everything we need," Sara replied, patting the camera on her lap.

Granger started the car and backed from the driveway to the main road.

It was a gorgeous, sunny day with a few fluffy clouds in the cerulean blue sky. Nothing could go wrong on a day like this, Sara thought. She chose some happy rock music on the radio while Granger headed toward the East Coast.

Sara had wanted to see the lighthouses so that was the reason why they went towards the coastline. Of course, attractions like Niagara Falls and the casino there were on their list, but they didn't plan to overnight there. A smaller place with cheaper hotel prices would suit their budget better. They had not made any reservations anywhere as they didn't know what they would see on their way there, and if they decided to take a detour to somewhere else. No restrictions on the travel plans were the best part. This was more like a honeymoon adventure than a planned trip.

The first part of the journey went smoothly, and they drove past the bigger cities where Sara took a few pictures of the shady sides of the cities with full trash containers, homeless people pushing their carts, and tent cities filled with either homeless or immigrants. As the day turned to evening, they stopped at a small and cozy roadside diner ate some burgers and slices of apple pie, and then continued their trip. It didn't matter where they went as long as the road ahead was not blocked with trucks and other traffic, and they could see different sites.

Three miles from the rest stop, they saw a sign for a motel with a vacancy sign lit on.

"Do you want to stay overnight here wherever we are now?" Granger asked.

"No, we can keep on going for a little bit longer."

"As you wish."

Chapter 2
The accident

As they drove along the highway, the sun was setting, and it was getting dark. They were close to the shoreline. Granger decided to drive ahead to get to the oceanside as the road ahead was clear, and they were on their own schedule, not expected anywhere.

Granger was driving. Not many passersby went by. It was a lonely highway at nighttime. The inky darkness swallowed the surroundings, with only the faint illumination of the van's headlights and the distant glow of stars piercing the black curtain. The hum of tires on the road became a tiresome and haunting tune in the darkness. The road stretched out endlessly, disappearing behind the hills and continuing again when you drove up the hill and descended it. The forest beyond the road seemed shrouded in thick bushes, trunks, and branches of nearby trees. Everything behind them was hidden from view.

Sara was curled in the passenger seat. She had her eyes closed, half asleep. Her long hair hung loose, covering her shoulders. Her camera was on the seat next to her.

Granger had his headlights on but was distracted as he fiddled with the radio station, causing him to miss a deer leaping out of the forest ahead. He slammed the brakes forcefully, but the deer collided with the front bumper, shattering the windshield and sliding over the car. Unfortunately, their aging minivan lacked airbags.

The abrupt halt sent Sara's camera tumbling to the floor, and her seatbelt prevented her from lurching forward due to the sudden stop. Meanwhile, Granger felt the seatbelt's strong resistance as it stopped him from colliding with the windshield. He knew he would be bruised and sore the next day in the shoulder and around his ribcage where the seatbelt injured him.

"Sara, are you okay?"

Sara nodded, rubbing her neck. "My neck hurts. Whiplash, maybe."

"Sorry about the crash. I hit a deer. It happened so fast that I just couldn't stop before I hit him." He opened the seatbelt, adding," I'll go outside to check up on our car and the deer."

He already knew the windshield was a mess, but he didn't expect to see the bloody carcass of a deer on the roadside, his neck twisted. The blood was splattered on the dented hood, which was partly ajar due to the impact. The car had a partially dislodged bumper and an apparent inward bend in the left tire. Additionally, the left side fender showed significant denting and was pressed against the tire. He rubbed his chin and looked around. A dark forest, with no signs of houses or towns anywhere. *What should we do?* he wondered. *We could call a tow truck, but we don't even know exactly where we are, I'm not sure I can drive this car further.*

I could try, but even if it starts, that left wheel and the fender will give me a hard time. It needs a mechanic to fix it.

The loud buzzing of cicadas and clicks and chirps of either bats or nocturnal birds added an eerie soundtrack to the scene, creating an otherworldly vibe. Granger was not a country boy, so whenever he heard a screech or a howl, he turned his head, trying to see into the darkness, but couldn't see what had caused the sound.

Sara opened the passenger side door and asked, "How does it look?"

"Not good."

Sara took a step forward and lifted her hand on her mouth as she saw the twisted body of the deer on the roadside. "Oh, we killed him."

Chapter 3
Where to Go?

"Have you checked your cell phone?" Sara asked as she pulled out hers and started fiddling with it. "I can't get any signal here. It's like we're off the map and out of reach of any satellites." She lifted her cell phone higher in the air and walked a few steps to get a better reception to her phone, but it had no bars or connection. "We can't call anyone to help."

"We're in the middle of the forest and hills, so that might block the cellphone reception," Granger replied.

"These nighttime sounds around us," Sara started, and her eyes surveyed the roadside. "Are they cicadas or something else? I hear buzzing and clicking sounds."

"Yes, it could be cicadas. There are nocturnal cicadas in certain areas, but most likely, they are crickets, katydids, or bats," Granger replied. Adding, "It's an unnerving sound, isn't it? The darkness, no humans or cars around, no light except the stars above, and the rhythmic buzzing sound."

Sara gave him a stern look. "Now you're making me scared of being here alone with a broken car," Sara said, hugging herself and shivering as the chilly night breeze penetrated her thin cardigan. "I'm going back inside the car."

Her eyes darted back to the dark forest engulfing the roadside. She was sure someone was watching them from over there. *Perhaps it's just my imagination,* she thought, although she was sure she saw movement behind the tree line. *It could be another deer or some other animal,* she thought. She sat back inside the car and closed the door.

With the nighttime cricket sounds, the world seemed to have changed into a deserted world with no humans, no buildings, and no lights. Their headlights were still on, but they only covered a short strip of the road ahead, leaving even darker shadows outside their perimeter.

Granger viewed the damage closer. The left side of the fender looked bad. He tried to pull it away from the tire but couldn't. *Can we even drive when it is pressing against the tire?*

He walked to the back of the car and took out a string. *At least I can tie that bumper, so it won't fall off when we drive,* he decided.

After doing that, he asked Sara, "Hand me a water bottle. I have to rinse my hands."

Sara pulled a bottle from behind the seat and handed it to him. He opened it, poured the water over his hands one after the other, and rubbed them together. And then poured some more. When he had got the blood rinsed away, he sat back inside.

"Let's try to start this again," Granger muttered more to himself than to Sara.

The engine kicked off without a hitch, but as soon as he hit the gas and began to drive, he sensed the left tire's struggle to turn. "Come on, don't let us get stranded out here," he muttered.

After a few tense seconds of pressing down on the gas pedal, the left tire finally moved, and the van jerked forward. The ride was far from smooth, with the right side behaving as expected while the left tire continued to struggle.

Their speed was slow as Granger tried to save the car so they wouldn't have to walk in the dark. He turned left from the highway, hoping to find a town and trying to avoid the fast-paced roads with the broken vehicle.

"Do you have any idea where we are?" Sara asked, staring at the dark road ahead.

"No, I don't know. I just kept going forward on the highway. I think we are close to the ocean, though," Granger replied. He hoped it was true because many villages were located there with the lighthouses that Sara wanted to see.

Behind the next curve, they saw a small village nestled at the water's edge, and a gravelly road led toward it.

"Finally, back into the civilization." Sara sighed.

"It's about time. I don't think this car would have lasted much longer," Granger said, heading down the hill leading to the village.

Chapter 4
The Village

THEY REACHED THE CLEARING in the middle of this quaint village, and the moon sailed free in the dark sky, bathing the buildings with pale light. Granger parked the car on the side of the clearing near the inn, and they stepped outside.

The stone and wood buildings, adorned with vintage hanging signs of inns and general stores, dangled from metal hooks, gently swaying in the breeze and emitting a subtle creaking sound with each sway. The buildings cast shadows so dark that Sara and Granger couldn't see what was between them.

The windows were all dark and closed with shutters.

"Where is everyone?" Sara inquired as she spun around, surveying the empty and shadowy-looking town.

"I don't see anyone," Granger admitted. "Scary."

"Is it so late that no one is awake?"

"I don't think so." Granger glimpsed at his smartwatch and furrowed his eyebrows. "My watch has stopped. I don't know what time it is."

Sara pulled out her cell phone from her purse. "My cellphone's clock has stopped. It shows 11:49, but that was probably the time of the accident."

"Could be, or it could be when we entered this Twilight Zone town," Granger commented.

"Don't say that." Sara swatted Granger on the arm. "It's already creepy enough without you making fun of it."

"Let's try the inn's door. We'll have to get a room and stay here until our car is fixed," Granger said, placing his arm around Sara's shoulders and pulling her toward the inn. The old-fashioned-looking building exuded an air of 'go away' charm with its stone walls that bore the weathered marks of time. The exterior, with creeping ivy and vintage unlit rusty lanterns, greeted visitors with an aura of the past century.

Granger tried to open the heavy wooden door, but it was closed. He knocked on the door. And took a step back to see if any lights came to the windows.

No movement. No lights. No sounds from inside. No one came to the door.

He banged the door harder and louder.

Finally, he heard some shuffling sounds inside. It sounded like someone had removed something from the front of the door, and a few seconds later, it cracked open.

The interior remained shrouded in darkness as the narrow crack offered no glimpse of the room behind the door.

Their view inside was completely obscured, leaving them unable to identify who had answered the door. Granger assumed it was a man, as the figure was as tall as he was.

Granger cleared his throat. "Good evening, sir. Our car broke down. We need a room. Do you have any vacancy?"

"Can't you leave this town?" a man's voice asked harshly.

Not a friendly place, Granger thought. "No, we had an accident and need a mechanic to fix our car. We'll probably have to stay in this charming little town for a few more days." Sarcasm showed through his words as he didn't consider this village charming, and their host here was anything but.

Sara tried her charm, smiling. "Please, we are really tired, and our car is a mess. Could you give us a room, sir?"

"If you must stay here... I guess I could rent you a room," the man replied reluctantly. He opened the door just enough for them to step inside and closed it with a bang after them. To their surprise, he pulled a heavy wooden bench in front of the door so no one could get in or out.

Chapter 5
The Inn

As Sara and Granger stood watching their host blocking the doorway, they exchanged glances, questioning what was happening. Why had he blocked the door like that? They didn't have to say it aloud, as it was as strange as the darkness inside that engulfed them. All the windows had closed shutters, and no candles or gas lights were lit. This wasn't a cozy countryside inn with a warm atmosphere. It was anything but.

A ridiculous, irrational fear rose inside Sara, and she pressed closer to Granger.

The disturbing atmosphere enveloped them.

The scent of smoke lingered in the air, hinting that the fireplace had been lit earlier but had since been extinguished.

Their host, a tall man with stooped shoulders wearing dark, old-fashioned clothes, said, "Come to the kitchen. I'll make something for you to eat. The room won't be ready for a while. You'll have time to eat."

He walked in the darkness as if he was used to doing that every day and night. Granger and Sara followed his dark form. He lit an oil lamp in the kitchen and placed it on a rickety wooden table. "Sit," he told them.

They pulled out two worn wooden chairs and sat down by the table.

At least now they could see what their host looked like. The faint glow of the oil lamp lit the kitchen area and their host. He was an elderly man with grey hair sprouting behind his large hairy ears. His nose was crooked, and he had a pointy chin. Sara wished she could take a picture of him, as he could be great as an old wizard. His straight pants were dark cotton, reaching barely to his ankles. He had dark shoes with pointy tips, and the sleeves of his coat reached past his elbows but not to his wrists. His stripy shirt had once been white, but now it was a shade of grey with darker grey stripes.

The man opened the refrigerator's door, and no light lit inside. He seemed to know what he was looking for as he reached inside and took out a carton of eggs, ham, half an onion, a boiled potato, a tomato, and a green pepper. He placed them next to the stove and cracked the eggs into a bowl, adding some spices. He sliced the tomato, ham, and tomato, poured the eggs into the frying pan and the other ingredients into the next pan and switched on the gas stove with a few clicks.

His actions were efficient, with short, energy-conserving movements, as if he had executed these motions countless times.

As Sara and Granger viewed the small kitchen in the soft, amber glow that made the shadows dance across the century-old stone walls, creating a spooky atmosphere. Wooden beams crisscrossed the low ceilings, adding rustic character to the small kitchen area. Soon, the scent of cooking onions and ham filled the air.

Granger felt his stomach growling. It had been hours since their last meal. The accident had taken place in the middle of nowhere, and the rest of the trip had been slow, mostly at a snail's pace, trying to keep the left tire turning and not breaking it while they were on the road. He grabbed Sara's hand under the table and squeezed it tight. She glanced at him, and he grinned. "We have a roof over our heads for tonight, and we don't have to spend our night in a broken car."

"Yes, you're right," Sara replied, relieved. Granger always knew how to make her feel better.

Their host turned, looking at them angrily. "Ssh!" He put his finger over his mouth, and his eyes darted around, scared.

Granger and Sara looked around the area but saw nothing alarming.

Their host held his breath and waited for something to happen, but when nothing did, he exhaled loudly and continued cooking, turning his back on the couple.

Granger turned to face Sara and lifted his eyebrows. Sara shrugged. *What is going on here? The man seems scared of something or afraid our voices would wake someone up,* Granger thought. Whatever it was, they better stay silent if that's what their host wanted.

When the omelet was ready, their host quietly took two plates from the cupboard and placed them in front of them. Next, he served them the omelet with expert moves. It was steaming hot, emitting an inviting scent of onions and pepper. He handed them forks and glasses filled with water and whispered, "I'll go make your room ready. Stay here. Be quiet. I will come back to get you." He tiptoed quietly out of the kitchen like a ghost, leaving them sitting by the table in the dim light of the oil lamp.

Chapter 6
The First Night

Sara rolled her eyes and whispered, "What was that all about?"

"I have no idea," Granger commented. "Let's eat before he returns."

They ate with gusto as the omelet tasted great, and they were both hungry as wolves. As soon as they finished, the odd man returned, gesturing for them to come after him. He grabbed the oil lamp from the table and led them upstairs. They had to stay close to him because he carried the only lit lamp, and they couldn't see much further than a few feet away. Behind that, the darkness engulfed everything. They only saw the next step of the winding staircase as they ascended to the second floor.

The man had left one door open. "That is your room," he mouthed quietly.

"How much does it cost?" Granger asked, realizing they didn't even know how much they would have to pay him.

"We'll talk about everything tomorrow morning," he said grimly, adding, "if you are still here."

"Why wouldn't we be here? Our car is broken, and we need to find a mechanic tomorrow," Sara replied, raising her voice.

"Sshh!" The man put his finger over his mouth and glared furiously at Sara, who stepped behind Granger.

He gestured to the open door, and Sara followed Granger inside. In the dim light of the gas lamp, they saw a large bed in the middle of the room and another door that led to the bathroom. As they viewed the room, their host backed out, leaving them in the dark. He closed the door after him, and both Sara and Granger heard a distinctive click on the lock.

"He locked the door," Sara murmured, grabbing Granger's hand.

"There's no light, not even candles," Granger commented. "Let's sleep now and figure out what to do tomorrow morning when it's light outside."

"Sure," Sara commented. "If you can sleep here. It's creepy."

They curled into the bed with their clothes on and fell asleep in minutes. The excitement and all that had happened to them had taken a toll.

Granger woke up sometime in the middle of the night. He wasn't sure what woke him, but he felt the urge to go to the bathroom. He got up quietly and went to the small bathroom adjoining their room, and after relieving himself, he was about to go to bed when he saw a crack letting in bright light through the boards that covered the window. Curious, he stepped to the window and peeked through the crack.

It was still night, but Granger didn't know the time. The moon was shining in the inky black sky. A few grey banks of cloud passed along the sky, covering the moon for a short time. In the moonlight, he saw that the shoreline was covered with strands of mist that seemed to swirl around figures, which he assumed were the residents of this village. *Do fishermen go out this early?* he wondered as he watched the scene unfolding before his eyes.

The ethereal figures emerged from the water, catching Granger's attention, and it was then that he realized they were transparent. Among them, a few bore a human resemblance, while others took on the forms of animals.

Discerning between the sexes of these beings was possible due to distinct features such as flowing dresses, pants, or long hair. Their eyes emitted an eerie glow, and they swiveled their heads as though searching for something or someone.

As Granger surveyed the village, he couldn't help but notice its profound darkness, devoid of any signs of life. It gave off an abandoned aura that enveloped everything.

Chapter 7
The Ghostly Creatures

EERIE AND OTHERWORLDLY, THESE ghostly figures emerged from the water one after another, their forms shimmering as they ascended from the water's embrace and walked after the first ones who already reached the inn where Granger was watching them.

Granger went to wake up Sara. "Shh!" He put his hand over Sara's mouth. He grabbed her hand and pulled her to the window to see the weird sight too. "What are they?" she whispered, mesmerized at the scene. "Are they ghosts?" She turned around to look for her camera, which she had left by the bedside. She walked there, took it, and returned to the window, pointing her camera at the scene. She didn't use the flash, afraid it would disturb the silent progression.

The creatures' translucent bodies seemed composed of liquid moonlight, casting an eerie glow around them as they floated toward the square, which was the same one where the inn was located.

Some of these phantoms wore billowing, archaic garments of past centuries. Others were not human but spectral felines and canines. Their fur was an ethereal mist, flowing like smoke, and it carried a faint, silvery shimmer that caught the moonlight. Ghost cats moved with mystic grace along the cobblestone pathways, and they appeared to effortlessly defy gravity, sometimes even floating a few inches above the surface. The outlines of these beings shifted and swirled, making it difficult to discern their true forms. Eyes that seemed to hold ancient mysteries glowed with an eerie light. They moved with a quiet purpose, their heads turning as though seeking answers hidden within the village's narrow and dark alleys.

As Granger and Sara kept watching the parade of ghosts, the village itself appeared frozen in time, enveloped in an eerie stillness. Stone cottages with thatched roofs stood like silent sentinels, their windows dark and empty. The cobblestone streets were worn smooth by centuries past, but now the ghostly parade took over and caused an otherworldly air to the once-charming seaside village.

Sara whispered, "Is this why our host wanted us to be quiet? He didn't want us to know about these ghosts, or he was afraid of these ghosts?"

"He seemed afraid of something," Granger mumbled, keeping his eyes on the ghosts.

One of them floated higher, a spectral feline, he guessed. His eyes gleamed from inside light that seemed to see through the walls. Granger withdrew back a bit, hoping that the cat wouldn't see him. However, the ghost cat seemed to have a sixth sense as he floated in front of their window, trying to see inside.

Granger lifted his finger on his lips, hinting to Sara to keep quiet. The ethereal feline passed their window a couple of times before he decided to leave.

Sara exhaled. "That cat seemed to know we were watching him."

"I'm sure he did. A cat can sense things." He gestured ahead. "Watch out! Ghost dogs are floating this way."

They both stepped back from the window and stood still.

Granger wasn't sure if their action was rational or not.

After a few minutes, he moved back to the window and glanced through the crack again. The spectral canines had floated past and not stopped, but that stubborn cat was circling back toward the inn in the opposite direction as the other ghosts!

When he was in front of their window, he pushed his head through it and appeared in their room. He paced between them like a normal cat, except his feet didn't reach the floor. He twined between their legs and circled them, acting like a regular cat.

Granger looked at Sara, raising his eyebrows as if to ask, *What should we do with him?*

Sara lifted her shoulders to this silent question, then raised her camera and took a few pictures of the ghost cat.

The cat's body tensed when he saw the camera in front of Sara's face. He hissed, and his luminous fur bristled. He unsheathed his sharp claws and scratched the air in between them. The camera had scared him. After a few seconds of staring at Sara, he jumped through the wall. Sara and Granger rushed to the window to see what would happen next, only to see the other ghosts gathering around the scared cat and then looking in the direction where he had come from.

And the ghosts started moving toward the inn.

The lock clicked as if someone had turned the key, then the door swung open, and their host materialized in the doorway. "What have you done?" His voice trembled with fear.

"I attempted to capture a photograph of the ghost cat," Sara offered in explanation.

"Oh dear," their host lamented, gently covering his eyes with his hand.

Chapter 8
The Ghosts Appear

EERIE AND OTHERWORLDLY, THE ghosts floated toward the inn. The innkeeper swore and scampered away, leaving Sara and Granger to deal with the unwelcome spooky guests.

The spectral creatures gathered in front of the inn as a group, with no distinct form merging, reminding Sara of a shimmering cloud. It was impossible to distinguish a single figure in the mass of ghosts; they seemed to move together as a weird entity.

"Are they dangerous?" Sara mouthed to Granger, keeping her eyes glued to the ghosts.

"Our host seems to fear them, so I guess we should hide," Granger replied, pulling her away from the window and into the small, windowless bathroom. He hoped it would be safe enough, although he was sure the ghosts could float through the walls and appear inside a locked room.

He locked the door, knowing well that it was unnecessary and futile.

Granger ushered Sara into the vintage claw-footed bathtub, and they hunkered down inside. He draped a sizable towel over their heads, whispering into Sara's ear, "Stay silent." They nestled together beneath the towel, praying that no ghosts would discover their hiding place.

An eerie silence settled in as a feeling of foreboding hung heavily in the air. An icy draft swept into the bathroom, even though there were no windows. Both of them held their breath, fearing that the sudden cold was a result of a ghostly presence.

They exhaled slowly and quietly to avoid attracting any ghost's attention. The ghosts seemed to exude an aura of bitterness and resentment, as if they harbored centuries-old grudges. Chilling, inhuman voices echoed through the rooms, laced with scorn and hostility, sending shivers down their spines.

Granger decided it was safe to peek from under the towel when the air seemed to warm up again.

A pair of radiant eyes stared at him, curious and surprised.

The ghost cat! Granger thought. *He must have sensed I was here.*

The cat's eyes were the most captivating feature. Even though the bathroom was dark, the ghost cat illuminated his vicinity, and Granger could study him more thoroughly. His eye color shifted from a soft blue to a burning, ethereal green. And they seemed to hold secrets of the afterlife as they pierced through the darkness of the bathroom with an eerie intensity.

The haunting cat opened his mouth to meow, but Granger put his finger over his mouth. He didn't want any loud sounds and hoped the cat knew the meaning of staying quiet.

The spectral feline pawed his arm, but it passed right through, sending a bone-chilling sensation coursing through him as the spectral paw made contact with his limb.

Granger dropped the towel and revealed Sara, too.

The ghost cat's gaze fixated immediately on Sara as if she were a peculiar or intriguing occurrence in this living world. His spectral eyes followed Sara's movements as she changed her position in the bathtub.

The ghost feline glared at them, veering his eyes from one human to the next. He tried to mimic the playful pouncing of a living cat, leaping at his prey, and tried to bat both of them with spectral paws. His curiosity manifested as faint, ghostly meows and purrs, barely audible but conveying his desire to engage and interact with humans he had not met before.

In a display of spectral curiosity, the phantom feline disappeared and reappeared, playing tricks on Granger and Sara, leaving behind a trail of enigmatic appearances.

Sara and Granger kept looking around, trying to guess where the ghost cat would appear next. He didn't seem malevolent but acted like a playful cat who wanted to be friendly with them. The ghost cat drifted through walls and passed the objects in the bathroom, seemingly exploring the environment from a spectral perspective, driven by their insatiable curiosity,

Both Granger and Sara kept quiet. They hoped that his action would not attract the other ghosts because some or all of them could be hostile toward living humans. Why else would the host disappear so fast? There had to be a reason for his fear of ghosts.

Chapter 9

The Ghosts Return to the Water

THE GHOST CAT GOT tired of playing with them as he couldn't touch them, and they couldn't interact with him, so he floated through the wall and vanished from sight.

Sara mouthed, "Is it safe to stand up? Can we return to our room?"

"Let me check." Granger stepped out of the bathtub as quietly as he could and went to the door. The air felt normal, with no cool breeze like when the ghosts had entered their room. Cautiously, he cracked the door open, surveying the surroundings for any spectral apparitions. Satisfied that the ghosts had departed without noticing them, he gestured to Sara, inviting her to follow.

Together, they tiptoed to the window where the panel was cracked and peeked outside. Sara touched the windowsill, and it felt freezing, still bearing the signs of the ghostly encounter.

The wan moon cast its gentle glow upon the shoreline, bathing the water in its ethereal glow. The streets were empty and dark except for the specters who floated around toward the square and coalesced there until turning toward the water from which they had appeared.

A band of spirits escorted an elderly man, his appearance disheveled in a tattered sleeveless t-shirt and underpants, barefoot and sockless. His hair stuck up as if he had just been roused. Sara and Granger kept watching the strange encounter: their attention was fixated on a lone human figure, compelled to accompany the ethereal entourage towards the shoreline and into the water.

"How do they make him walk with them?" Sara whispered in astonishment.

"Possibly through some form of telepathy. That man appears terrified and coerced," Granger replied, his gaze unwavering as he tracked the ghostly procession. "He's their prisoner."

"The ghosts are immaterial. I don't understand how they can force the man to go with them," Sara kept asking.

"Look! The ghosts are merged into the solid wall of transparent mass, and that mass is pushing the man deeper into the ocean. They are going to kill him," Granger said.

Whitecapped waves lapped at the shore, and the man continually glanced back in search of salvation, finding none. His eyes were wide in terror. He called for help, but no one replied.

The ethereal procession of ghosts moved with eerie grace toward the water's edge, their transparent bodies shimmering in the pale moonlight. As they reached the shoreline, a strange and otherworldly ritual began to unfold.

One by one, the ghosts separated from the mass, dipping their incorporeal feet into the water, sending ripples of spectral energy across the surface. Their movements were slow and deliberate, as if they were communing with the very essence of the water. As more and more of them ventured further in, the water seemed to react, its surface becoming an otherworldly mirror to their ghostly forms.

A transformation occurred as the spirits continued to wade deeper into the dark water. Their ghostly outlines began to blur and merge with the water, coalescing into a single, undulating mass of transparent energy covering the surface around the man. It was a mesmerizing sight, as if they were becoming one with the very substance they traversed.

The once-clear boundary between the ghostly realm and the ocean depths blurred and faded. With each passing moment, it became increasingly challenging to discern where the spirits ended and the water began. It was a bizarre fusion of two entities, the ghosts and the aquatic.

Then, in the final moment, the fused entity of ghosts and water submerged beneath the surface. As they descended, the moonlight played upon the water, casting an eerie, dancing glow upon the liquid depths of the ocean. The ripples and disturbances that the ghost entourage and the man had caused slowly dissipated, leaving no trace of their presence on the water's surface. Everything returned to a calm nightly view of the ocean bathing in the moonlight.

"That was weird," Sara said. Sara remarked. "He walked willingly to his doom. And the ghosts mingled with the water and then dissipated."

"Yes, an odd union of the ghosts and the water. I guess the ghosts sought one human sacrifice tonight. Fortunately, it wasn't one of us," Granger replied, relieved, and put his arm around Sara's shoulders.

Chapter 10
The Rest of the Night

THE REMAINDER OF THE night unfolded in complete silence, devoid of the spectral manifestations that had initially sent shivers down Granger and Sara's spines. Despite the absence of ghostly apparitions, an unshakable unease lingered in the air.

In the dimly lit room, Granger and Sara devised a cautious strategy to ensure their safety, uncertain about the events that had transpired earlier. With an abundance of caution, they agreed to take turns watching and guarding while the other one slept in the bed. This way, they reasoned, at least one of them would be vigilant, ready to respond to any unexpected ghostly intrusions.

The decision to maintain this watchful vigilance was driven by fear and uncertainty. They couldn't comprehend the intentions of the spirits they had witnessed that night, nor could they fathom the depths of their powers. Did the ghost communicate telepathically? Was that how they forced the poor man to go with them? They had no idea. The mysterious merging of ghosts with water had left them with more questions than answers, and the enigma gnawed at their minds.

As Granger kept a watchful eye, the room was bathed in the soft glow of the moonlight filtering through the curtains, creating an ethereal ambiance that heightened his senses. The minutes ticked away slowly, and the weight of the night pressed upon him, leaving him worried and puzzled.

Each creak of the old house in the wind, every rustle of the branches in the breeze outside, sent a shiver down his spine as if the very night itself held secrets he was not meant to comprehend. In those quiet hours, his imagination ran wild, conjuring all manner of ghostly scenarios and supernatural possibilities. What if the ghosts returned and took one of them or both of them with them into the depths of the ocean? Was there anything they could do?

But the night remained still, save for the subtle sounds of the wind and the waves lapping on the shoreline. No new ghosts materialized, and no eerie whispers echoed in the dark. It seemed that the ghosts had left behind only a haunting memory.

As the first light of dawn streamed through the curtains, casting aside the cloak of darkness, Granger woke up Sara and finally allowed himself to close his eyes for a couple of hours. The ordeal of the night had left them physically and emotionally drained, but the unanswered questions still haunted their minds.

After a short sleep, Granger woke up. His eyes darted around the room, and he sighed as his gaze met Sara's slim figure sitting by the window, still keeping an eye on the ghosts. When she heard him moving, she turned her head and gave him a tired smile. "Good morning."

"Good morning." Granger sat up and rubbed his face. He felt utterly drained of any energy. The night, with all the excitement and fear, had exhausted him.

In the pale morning light, they exchanged weary glances, silently acknowledging the unspoken understanding that they had ventured into a twilight zone village where the boundary between the living and the spectral was perilously thin.

With a heavy sigh, Sara commented, "I know last night's encounter with the ghosts is far from over. Our car is broken. Can we leave this village even if we try?"

"I don't have an answer for you, but I do know that I will spend the rest of the morning and the day looking for a mechanic who can fix our car as fast as possible, and if that's not doable, then we'll find a rental car and leave our vehicle here." He stood up and extended his hand. "Let's go downstairs and find our host and see if he can explain to us what happened last night."

Sara nodded, stood up, stretched her arms, and then walked to him. "Perhaps we can also have some breakfast," she added, grabbing his hand and squeezing it tight.

Granger pulled her closer and kissed her. And with their molten kiss, the terrors of the night dissipated, leaving only a haunting memory of the ghost cat and his companions.

Chapter 11
At Breakfast

GRANGER TOOK THE LEAD, carefully descending the old, wooden, and worn staircase with Sara in tow carrying her camera.

The transition from the scary darkness of the previous night to the welcoming embrace of daylight was striking. As they made their way down, the inn seemed almost unrecognizable in the cheerful morning sun, which streamed in through windows that had been previously barricaded.

The innkeeper, an enigmatic man they had only glimpsed briefly the night before, had taken down the boards hastily nailed over the windows, allowing the warm, golden rays of the sun to flood the space.

The resulting illumination unveiled the inn's rustic charm, casting long, inviting shadows across the polished wooden floors.

Sara glanced around, viewing the charming inn now that she could finally see the inside properly. When they arrived last night, it had been so dark she couldn't see anything. Now, her eyes darted around the inn's first floor, where the sunlight dabbled a soft, amber glow across the centuries-old stones in the walls, creating an intimate and timeless atmosphere. Wooden beams crisscrossed the low ceilings, adding rustic character to the space.

The air was saturated with the inviting aromas wafting from the kitchen, a tantalizing blend of sizzling ham, freshly cooked eggs, and the rich, comforting fragrance of brewed coffee.

The lobby area had antique chandeliers, several worn wooden tables, and plush, velvet-upholstered chairs.

The inn's fireplace served as the heart of the inn, and Sara could imagine how inviting the room would be when the fire was lit, radiating gentle warmth and casting playful shadows on the ancient tapestries that adorned the walls.

"This is beautiful. I want to take some pictures after we've had breakfast," Sara commented excitedly.

Granger gave her a weak smile. "We'll see how long we stay here. I don't want to spend another night in this village if we can avoid it."

"Sure. I also want to ask the innkeeper if I can feature his inn in my next exhibition," Sara added as they stepped down from the last step of the stairs and headed to the kitchen.

The winding stairs, now bathed in sunlight, emitted familiar creaks that had gone unnoticed in the obscurity of the previous night. These sounds, however, proved to be an unintentional alarm, signaling their coming to their host. A door to the kitchen was ajar, and a curious face cautiously peered at them, his features bathed in the morning light. "Good morning," he greeted them, his tone carrying a touch of relief.

"It seems you've made it through the night in this peculiar village."

Sara went straight to the business asking, "Do you mind if I take more pictures of your inn? I'd like your permission to use the photos in my next photograph exhibit."

"Yes, I'd be delighted," the innkeeper replied smiling. "My family has lived here for centuries, and this place has seen so much." His gaze turned somber when he added, "Not all my memories are pleasant, though."

Granger and Sara exchanged a glance, their experiences from the night before still fresh in their minds. The innkeeper's comment reminded them of the unsettling events they had witnessed, and it hung in the air, unspoken yet palpable.

Granger grabbed Sara by the hand and led her to the kitchen.

They sat at the table just like they had done the previous night.

Their host filled two plates for them and poured steaming hot coffee into their cups. He had scrambled eggs, and their yolks, a vibrant yellow, glistened on the plates. Neatly nestled beside the eggs, slices of savory ham exuded a smoky aroma, and a couple of golden-brown toast slices completed their breakfast. The jelly and marmalade were in glass jars with handwritten labels hinting they were homemade, not purchased from a store.

Their host had large bags under his eyes, and his face looked haunted. He wore a long-sleeved shirt and dark pants just like last night, but now he had a long white apron on. He sat on a stool next to the stove, waiting for his guests to finish their breakfast.

Granger and Sara tasted the eggs, noticing the fresh flavor. The toast with jam was also delicious. After eating, Sara said, "Thank you. This breakfast was delicious."

Granger leaned back on the chair, and his eyes met the innkeeper's as he said, "Tell us what you know about the ghosts last night."

The man paled. "You don't want to know." He fidgeted with the hem of his apron. "You better leave this place while you can."

Chapter 12
The story behind the ghosts

Granger and Sara exchanged uneasy glances as unease settled over them. Granger broke the silence, his voice tinged with concern. "This situation is starting to feel rather strange, don't you think?"

Sara, though perplexed, offered a nonchalant shrug. But Granger, his curiosity piqued, wasn't about to let it go. "We can't afford to be in the dark here. Our car is kaput, and we're stuck here for at least another night. It could be longer if we can't find a mechanic to fix it."

The innkeeper's countenance shifted, growing notably displeased. He leaned in closer, his voice quivering. "You two shouldn't be here. You must leave –

now. Walk, run, do whatever it takes to put distance between you and this place. I'm not joking. Staying in this village is not safe."

Sara's eyes widened with apprehension, and she pleaded, "But you have to explain. We can't just abandon our car and all our belongings. We're in the middle of a month-long road trip, planning to capture the sights of different cities and attractions through our photographs. We need our car fixed so we can continue our adventure."

The innkeeper pulled a chair for himself and sat down, preparing to reveal a long-buried secret. "All right, let me start from the very beginning. My name is Walter Katz. My family has been rooted in this village for generations, and what I'm about to tell you dates back half a century." He paused, a heavy sigh escaping him as he rubbed his weary face with trembling hands. "It was a stormy night. I recall it like it happened yesterday. I had never seen the sea so dark and menacing as it was that night. It roared with relentless fury; its surface churned into a frothy turmoil. Towering waves, monstrous in scale, rose like giants from the depths of the sea. I remember thinking as I watched the waves crashing to the shoreline that their crests, the whitecaps, gleamed ominously in the dim moonlight. It was as if the whole sea was rising and heading toward us. All of us villagers had heard the warnings of the storm hitting the coastal line, and we had prepared for it, but we were not prepared enough. The monstrous storm was stronger than anyone expected." He paused and shook his head. "We didn't know that our shoreline was so fragile. The ground had eroded under the seaside part of the village, and when the enormous waves hit the shoreline and reached the houses, they pulled half the village with them into the abyss, never to be seen again." His gaze met Granger's as he added, "And that's when this ghostly horror began."

"What do you mean?" Granger asked, although expected to hear that it had something to do with the half of the village that was pulled into the depths of the sea.

"The villagers, including the animals who drowned that night, came back every night after that night. And every time they take one living being away with them... if they can find one. That's why the rest of us here try to stay quiet, keep out the lights, and don't make any sounds, hoping they will pass our house and leave us alone. Because if you make a sound, you'll commit yourself to the horrible death of drowning. The ghosts will grab you and pull you into the underwater village with them."

"The village is still there?" Sara asked, gasping in horror, her eyes wide.

"Yes, it's still there. If you take a boat and sail a bit further out, you can see the buildings underwater."

Chapter 13
The Decision to Stay in the Village

SARA GLANCED AT GRANGER and said, "I want to see that village." She faced Walter Katz and asked, "Mr. Katz, can we rent a boat? I'd like to see the underwater village or what's left of it. Is it safe to go out there?"

Walter Katz raised his eyebrows. "You should leave this village as soon as possible. Nothing is safe here. I just told you why."

Granger knew his wife. When Sara got the idea of a photograph, she would go to the ends of the Earth to take it. He saw the gleam in her eyes.

Granger knew there was nothing he could do to change her mind. Thus, he lifted his shoulders and repeated Sara's question, "Where can we find a boat? We'll just take a quick tour out to the open sea and see what we can uncover."

Walter Katz stood up, offering a solution. "You can borrow my ship. She is docked by the pier down by the shoreline. Her name is Turbo. I'll prepare a meal for you upon your return. You'll still have ample time to depart thereafter."

"We'll see about that," Sara muttered under her breath.

Granger knew his stubborn wife. He recognized her desire to linger, to delve deeper into the mysteries of the ghostly apparitions haunting this forsaken village. She yearned to uncover the enigma behind their nightly return.

Before they set off, Granger had one more question on his mind. "There's something we noticed last night—a ghostly apparition of a cat. It's quite surprising to think that even cats can become ghosts. Was that cat among those that perished that fateful night?"

Walter nodded solemnly. "Indeed, it was my father's cat, a mischievous feline named Minx. When my father's home succumbed to the sea, the cat met the same fate. I never laid eyes on them alive again. I've tried peering through the gaps in the boarded-up windows in hopes of spotting my father among the spectral figures, but the crowd is so numerous, and they move as one. It's a challenge to discern any individual among them. Besides, I dare not linger by the window too long; I fear drawing the attention of the ghosts."

Sara extended her condolences, her voice laced with empathy. "It must be truly heartbreaking to think that your father's spirit can't find rest after perishing in such a horrible and unexpected way."

The innkeeper's expression grew somber as he affirmed her words. "Indeed, it is," he acknowledged, his gaze shifting towards Granger. "We used to have a local car repair shop in this town, run by a man named Murkinson. His shop still stands, but I can't say for certain if he's among the missing now. Each day, the ghosts claim another soul in our village."

Granger, determined to resolve their car troubles, expressed his gratitude. "Thank you for your assistance," he said, rising from his seat. "We'll make a brief trip and be back by noon, I believe." Sara joined him as they left the inn.

As they descended the staircase leading to their room, Sara couldn't contain her excitement, whispering to Granger, "This is so thrilling!" She ensured her camera was ready, verifying the presence of extra memory cards and anticipating the opportunity to capture the unbelievable sights of a ghost village.

Granger, ever the pragmatist, nodded in agreement. "It should be safe to set sail. The ghosts tend to confine their wanderings to the nighttime hours. Plus, the weather outside is sunny, promising an ideal day for venturing out to sea." He held the door open for Sara, and once they were inside, he added, "But keep in mind, I still need to find a mechanic for our car. I can't just leave it here unattended."

"Sure. "We'll go to visit the local car repair shop first thing before sailing," Sara assured him, leaning towards his muscular chest and giving him a passionate kiss.

Chapter 14
The Ghost Village during Daylight

Sara and Granger walked hand in hand through the village, finding the local car repair shop still open. Murkinson was alive. Granger sighed in relief as he approached the man in coveralls and said, "Mr. Murkinson? We are staying at the inn, and Mr. Katz said you could help us repair our car. It broke down nearby, and we don't want to leave it behind."

Murkinson was in his fifties with greying hair and a large mustache. He turned around, and both Sara and Granger could see the sorrow and tiredness etched in his eyes and the deep wrinkles of his face. "Yes, how can I help you?" He wiped his hands with a stained towel and approached them.

"We had an accident on the road a few miles from here. I hit a deer, and the car's front and left side were badly bent. I could barely drive it here. Could you fix it for us? It's parked on the square in front of the inn where we are staying," Granger explained hastily.

"I can take a look at it. We don't have much business here. It's been a slow year," Murkinson admitted. "I guess you saw why if you stayed in the inn last night."

"If you mean the ghosts, then yes, we saw them," Granger replied.

"Okay, I'll take my tow truck and swing by the inn and bring your car here and take a look at it. I'll drop by later this afternoon to give you an estimate," Murkinson responded.

"Thank you, Mr. Murkinson," Granger said, placing his hand on Sara's shoulders. They left the repair shop and headed to the shoreline. They returned to their vehicle and took out their snorkeling gear because they would need it when they dived underwater and Sara took pictures there.

They found Mr. Katz's ship. It was a fairly new-looking fiberglass ship with an open cabin. It could probably be a way to earn more money during the tourist season, except with ghosts, that would not happen in this village. Granger suspected the previous owner might have gone with the ghosts and left the boat for the innkeeper. Katz had kept it in good condition, perhaps hoping to earn more income when the ghosts were gone.

Sara and Granger climbed onboard the ship, departing from the odd village where the eerie apparitions had materialized the previous night. Their destination was the enigmatic underwater ghost village shrouded in mystery and intrigue.

As they pushed off from the shoreline, it felt as if the nightly ghost parade was just a bad dream and nothing more. The sun hung high in the azure blue sky, coloring the surface of the sea with its golden rays. There was hardly any wind, and the sea looked calm.

The water was clear, and it was easy to see the bottom of the water near the shore, but when they got deeper, it was harder to discern any changes under the ever-changing blue and green colors.

Granger manned the helm, his steady hands guiding their vessel toward the deeper area where he suspected the village lay. "We didn't exactly ask where the village is located, but it can't be very far from the shoreline," Granger commented. "We don't know where the village's end was when it sank into the sea. The sea level could have risen after that storm, covering part of the land. When we get deeper, we'll start looking around."

Her camera in hand, Sara eagerly scanned down to the bottom of the sea, anticipation coursing through her veins as she imagined the ghostly village awaiting them beneath the waves.

As they ventured farther from the shoreline, Sara took a few pictures of the village they had left behind, its quaint cottages and narrow streets standing alone on the shoreline.

"Stop!" Sara shouted at Grainger, who slowed down and stopped.

"Did you see something?" he asked.

"I think I saw a formation underwater," Sara replied, staring down where she thought she had seen a change in the bottom of the sea.

They could feel the history and the presence of the ghostly village lurking beneath the surface, just waiting to be unveiled.

Granger dropped anchor, and the boat gently swayed on the undulating surface of the sea. He approached Sara and peeked down to the sea. "It's hard to see anything. Are you sure you saw something down there?"

"Yes, look over there," she pointed at a spot closer to the boat's shadow. "I think I can see a tower and a building there."

"You're correct. The shade makes it easier to distinguish the shapes of the bottom of the sea," Granger agreed. "We have the snorkeling gears, so we can go down there and see if you're correct."

They donned snorkeling gear and descended into the crystal-clear waters, where a surreal world awaited them.

Beneath the waves, the ghostly village came into view. Once vibrant and bustling, the village was now structures covered with greenish growth and stood as spectral remnants of a forgotten time. The play of sunlight on the surface created an otherworldly ambiance, casting dancing shadows upon the submerged ruins.

Granger and Sara floated in silent wonder, capturing the haunting beauty of the ghost village through their lenses. Sara took multiple pictures while they explored the eerie remains. They couldn't help but ponder the secrets and stories hidden within the watery depths, marveling at the condition of the buildings that stood there even though half a century had passed.

They saw a submerged church with a tower and a bell still attached. A school of fish swam by, alerted by the newcomers. Sara was excited as she got great shots of the fish and the old buildings.

Then, the spectral cat appeared.

"Minx!" Sara whispered as she stared at the ethereal being gazing at them from one of the windows.

Chapter 15
The Ghost Cat and the Village

SARA AND GRANGER SWAM closer to Minx, whose shiny eyes seemed to glow eerily. In the depth of the sea, his eye color was more yellowish than the green they had seen the previous night. His tail twitched as they moved closer, and seemed to watch them with eerie intensity.

Sara took a few pictures of the ghost cat while he near the window. Although a ghost probably didn't sit but rather floated above the window opening.

Amid the submerged ruins of the ghostly village, Granger and Sara found themselves staring at the cat that floated in front of them, then slowly vanished from their sight, only to reappear a few feet ahead.

Its translucent fur fluffed gently in the underwater currents; its eyes shone with an otherworldly gleam. The ghostly feline didn't approach them directly, but it seemed to lead them toward something he wanted them to see in the ruins of his submerged home.

Sara and Granger exchanged glances, and Sara shrugged as if she wasn't sure what to do: should they follow the ghost cat or leave him be? Sara was certain that this spectral cat had to be Minx because he looked the same as the one the last night. She swam ahead, following the fluid movements of the ghost.

The spectral cat bounced in front of them playfully and turned his head to make sure they were following him.

Sara reached out her hand, her fingers passing through the ghostly cat's form. Yet, the feline presence remained undaunted, and he nuzzled her hand in a manner that felt undeniably affectionate. Granger, equally captivated, extended his hand, and the transparent cat floated gracefully through his extended hand and floated between them as if attempting to bridge the divide between the living and the spectral.

In its otherworldly way, the ghost cat seemed to be extending an invitation, an offer of companionship beneath the waves. Granger and Sara faced each other and nodded as if agreeing to follow the spectral being, acknowledging the surreal but heartwarming encounter they were experiencing. They accepted the ghost cat's silent gesture to explore the underwater ruins together, united by a shared curiosity.

Minx led them to see the underwater garden, which had thrived since the village had submerged.

Aquatic plants had grown and taken on surreal forms and colors in this mystical garden. Seaweed swayed gently in the currents, its fronds adorned with a mesmerizing array of hues, from deep emerald greens to vibrant purples and blues. Some plants glowed with ethereal bioluminescence, casting a soft, ethereal glow that added to the garden's magical ambiance.

Amidst the swaying seaweed, they encountered a profusion of exotic and delicate coral formations. These living sculptures came in a kaleidoscope of colors, from the fiery oranges and reds of fire coral to the delicate pastels of soft corals.

Sara gestured to the corals and shook her head, trying to tell Granger that this should not exist here. She quickly took some pictures with the corals and the seaweed garden before they swam ahead.

The garden's inhabitants added to its grotesque mysticism. When Granger and Sara ventured ahead, they found the recently captured, missing persons from the village. They were tied onto poles like scarecrows in the middle of the field that seemed to present the crop field for the ghosts. The schools of vivid fish swam by the dead bodies, picking their flesh, their eyes already gorged out, and their clothes tattered.

Sara screamed or tried to, except her scream died in the depths of the ocean. She turned around and quickly started paddling away. Granger grabbed her by the leg and stopped her. He motioned toward her camera, telling her to take pictures of this, too. Sara's hands shook as she lifted the camera and took shots of the horrible field of nightmares.

The ghost cat sat by the first body, a male in his forties staring at them with his dead eyes. *He must have been the one taken the last night,* Granger thought.

Why did Minx show us this? he wondered. *Is there something behind all this?*

Chapter 16
Back in the Ship

SARA AND GRANGER HASTILY returned to the ship and removed their snorkeling gear.

"What in the world was that down there? The field with the dead bodies?" Sara spat out, her face looking gray.

Granger looked pensive. "I've read ghost stories, real and fiction, and one thing came into my mind. What if the ghosts taken so suddenly in that storm try to replace themselves with the living? What if when they died, they were trapped down there in a time-loop from which they can't escape or move forward."

"Do you believe that Minx is trying to tell us that?" Sara sat down and stared at Granger. "And what is exactly a time-loop you mentioned?"

"A time loop is exactly what it says: time loops over and over again. Same events will repeat, or a specific sequence of events will happen in the same order endlessly, and those trapped in that loop can't escape from their time prison," Granger explained. "What I don't understand is why the ghost cat wanted us to see it. Is he hoping us to end the time loop and help them to move on?"

Sara's response was hesitant, her voice quivering as she spoke, "Perhaps... I don't know. It was... creepy down there." An involuntary shiver rippled through her body as she recalled the unsettling experience.

"I'm cold," she added, her teeth chattering audibly, a clear sign of the chill that had settled into her bones.

Granger, concerned for her well-being, immediately sprang into action. "Or you might be in shock," he suggested, his voice laced with worry. "Let me get you a blanket from inside the cabin. Stay right here; I'll be back in a moment." Without waiting for a response, he hurried indoors, his footsteps echoing in the stillness surrounding them. There was no trace of wind, and the vast expanse of the sea lay before them in all directions, utterly undisturbed. The horizon was empty, devoid of any other ships, and the maritime landscape appeared desolate, like the last vessel adrift in an abandoned world.

Amid this eerie tranquility, the absence of sound was equally striking. No car engines hummed in the distance, and the wind carried no distant laughter or conversations. The world had fallen into an uncanny hush, a silence so complete that it felt as though they were the sole inhabitants of this secluded place.

Returning swiftly from the cabin, Granger draped a large, cozy blanket around Sara's trembling shoulders. As he tucked it snugly, he pulled her closer to him, providing both warmth and comfort. His gentle hands rubbed her back and arms, generating friction to stave off the cold that had taken hold.

After a few moments, Sara's teeth ceased clattering, and she murmured, her voice distant and contemplative, "A time loop..."

The words hung in the air between them; it was as though Granger had offered them a haunting piece of the puzzle that had eluded them and the living villagers until this moment, and it left Granger and Sara pondering the chilling possibility of the unending cycle they had unwittingly stumbled into.

"The only way to stop a time loop is to find a way for the ghost to move forward," Granger commented, still rubbing Sara's arms. Her face had some color now and she looked better.

"So, how can we stop it? Is there a way to stop it?" Sara asked, turning her face, who leaned closer and kissed her gently before answering. "I don't know if there is a way to stop it."

Chapter 17
The Time Loop

Sara inhaled deeply and tried to get rid of the ugly sights still lingering in her mind of the ghostly field with people as scarecrows.

Granger was quiet. Sara turned to face him and furrowed her eyebrows. "What is it?"

"When we entered this village, we might have entered into the time loop where the events repeat over and over again. I don't know if we can leave this place even if we try. Last night, we became part of the village even if we didn't know it. I believe the ghost cat wanted to greet us last night as if we were now amongst the villagers."

"We need to ask Walter Katz if anyone has left the village," Sara said. "Let's go back to the inn. He might have more answers for us."

"Yes, that's probably a good idea," Granger said, standing up and heading to the cabin to start the engine. Soon, they were on their way back to the shoreline. They tied the ship back to the pier and climbed on the wooden pier.

Sara had her camera hanging around her neck, and she held Granger by the hand as they walked back to the inn. "Tell me, what do your previous readings suggest doing with a time loop?"

"You have to find out why the time loop happened." Granger looked pensive. "The ghosts might have unfinished business or want revenge for some reason." He faced Sara and added, "We don't know what it could be because we never lived here. I think the only person who can help us is the innkeeper who has lived here all his life and so has his family before him. He must have some answers to stop all this."

When they reached the inn, Walter Katz was there in the lobby. He glimpsed at them when they walked in. "Good afternoon," he said. "Your lunch is ready when you are." He took a note from the table and handed it to Granger. "Your car repair estimate. If you want Murkinson to start working, I can go and tell him that while you eat."

Granger glanced at the bill. It wasn't so expensive. It was less than what he expected. "Yes, thank you. If he could hurry with it, I'd appreciate it."

"Sure. I'll let him know." Walter took off his apron and gestured to the table. "Do you want to have your lunch here or in the kitchen? Either way is fine with me."

"We can eat here," Sara decided and sat down by the table, placing her snorkel gear on the floor. She took off her camera and placed it on the table.

Granger gazed at Walter Katz and said, "We'd like to speak with you first before you go to the car repair shop if that's all right with you?"

"Yes, of course. Let me grab your plates from the kitchen." Walter disappeared and returned after a few minutes carrying two plates, which he placed in front of them. He had made Shrimp Scampi sautéed in garlic, butter, white wine, and herbs, served over a bed of linguine pasta. He returned to the kitchen and brought them the village's cider to drink.

He pulled a chair and sat next to their table. "What is it that you wanted to ask?"

Sara glanced at Granger and then pushed the camera toward him. Granger turned his eyes to Walter and asked, "Has anyone visited the underground village after it slid to the sea?"

"No, of course not. It feels... creepy to go there to see what is left of the buildings and the loved ones who used to live here," Walter said. "You didn't know any of them who died in that storm. We all lost someone back then. If you have some macabre images of the remains of our village underwater, then I don't want to see them."

Granger sighed. "Yes, we took some images, but that's not what we want to talk about."

"What is it then?" Walter looked suspicious.

"First, let me ask you one more question: Has anyone ever left this village and moved away?"

"No, never." Walter shook his head.

"Has anyone ever tried to leave this place?"

"No, I don't think so. I don't recall anyone leaving," Walter replied, looking puzzled. "Why do you ask?"

"Because I think the villagers who died in that storm are trapped in a time loop, and they have to repeat the unfortunate events, and they can't stop what they do. Also, I believe that these nightly visits to this village are because the ghosts are capturing living humans, and it is their way of trying to break free from their entrapment by attempting to replace themselves with the living. The ghosts may not fully understand the consequences of their actions, and their attempts to interact with the living world inadvertently result in the death of these captured people. They place the captured ones from here in the field like scarecrows." Granger watched keenly as the innkeeper listened to his story and paled. The mention of the dead as scarecrows made Walter sniff and bury his face in his hands.

"I didn't know. I swear I didn't know any of that," he mumbled. When he looked up, he had a haunted look on his face.

"What exactly you didn't know?" Sara asked, picking up something in his voice that wasn't just sorrow but also guilt. She pushed away her plate without touching the food. The topic was more interesting than eating.

Granger let his plate be as he stared at the innkeeper. "What is it? Tell us. We are as much in trouble here as you villagers are. I don't believe we can leave this place if this whole village is trapped in a time loop. We were able to enter, but I don't think this entrapment will allow us to leave until this time loop is solved."

Chapter 18
Walter's Story

"I swear, I had no idea," Walter kept repeating. His shaky hands patted his grey hair, and he lowered them back to the table.

"Tell us, please," Sara said gently.

Walter lifted his gaze and met her eyes, seeing she was seriously concerned. "Miss, I'm sorry you got entangled with our problems," he started, leaning back on his chair and rubbing his face. He took a deep breath and let it slowly out to calm himself. "We never gave them any burial. The church disappeared with them in that storm. We were all so devastated with the loss of our family members that we never set up any graveyard or tried to give them a proper burial in a sacred ground."

"You can do that still. It's not too late," Granger commented.

"That's not all." Walter turned his tormented gaze to Granger. He looked like had wanted to tell his story for a long time and get it off his chest. He started, "It's my fault that the land slid to the sea. I had made a deal with Geomine, a geothermal energy company. They drilled deep wells to tap into the Earth's crust for geothermal energy production. Drilling was necessary to access the hot rocks beneath the Earth's surface, and thus, they created fractures in the rock to enhance geothermal productivity." He paused and stared at the distance as if remembering the past. "I was just a young man back then. I didn't know that the ground was so fragile. The fractures caused the village to split, and when the storm hit with enormous waves, it pulled apart this village, and half of it sank into the sea. It was all my fault. My father died in that storm." Walter shook his head and added, "I never knew I would cause the death of so many people with my business idea. I swear I didn't know it would do that."

Granger glimpsed at Sara and commented. "Now we know why the ghosts are returning. My guess is that part of the reason is that they never got the real burial, and the other reason is the revenge because of Walter's business. They keep coming back until this is solved." He turned his eyes to Walter and asked, "Do you understand what I just said?"

Walter nodded. "I will have to pay for my deeds. A sacrifice."

"Yes, but we'll also have to make sure that the dead villagers get a real burial."

Granger kept his eyes on Walter, who nodded. "I understand."

"Why did they make scarecrows of the people they took from this village?" Sara asked.

Granger leaned in thoughtfully, his gaze fixed on distance as he recalled the scarecrows in the underwater depths. "Scarecrows resemble humans," he mused aloud, his voice carrying the weight of contemplation. "And in this extraordinary circumstance, they were real humans." His words hung in the air, punctuating the profound strangeness of their discovery.

He continued, his tone reflecting a deepening insight. "Humans are, by nature, vulnerable beings," Granger remarked. "I suppose that's what the ghosts intended to convey with this unsettling underwater tableau—our lives, no matter how vivid or enduring, are ultimately short and fragile. We, too, are susceptible to the inexorable passage of time, just as these scarecrows stand as reminders of that vulnerability."

His gaze shifted from Sara to Walter as if trying to draw a connection between the past and the present. "Yet," Granger went on, "there seems to be more to this haunting message. It's not merely a reflection of our mortality but a haunting testament to injustice." He paused, his words chosen carefully. "They blame Walter, and by extension, this village, for their unresolved fate. The ghosts' anger and sorrow stem not only from being left unburied but also from Walter's business venture, which inadvertently led to their untimely and unfortunate demise."

The words hung in the air like a lingering presence, as if the ghosts themselves sought to convey their message through Granger's voice. At this moment, beneath the waves, the scarecrows and the spectral souls that inhabited the submerged village appeared and stopped, staring upwards as if silently witnessing the events unfolding in the inn and Walter's confession, their silent, ghostly forms echoing an unsettling truth about the intertwined fates of the villagers above and beyond the sea.

Chapter 19
How to Stop the Ghosts

WALTER SAT WATCHING HIS two guests, his countenance marked by fear and deep-seated concern. In a voice tinged with uncertainty and vulnerability, he implored, "I find myself at a loss—unsure of the right course of action. What should I do in this situation?"

Granger responded thoughtfully, his brow furrowing in contemplation. "Give me a moment to mull it over," he requested, and with that, he began to eat his meal. Watching his pensive expression, Sara followed suit and brought her plate closer. The food before them was nothing short of delicious, and she found herself pleasantly surprised by her own appetite, a result, no doubt, of the energy expended during their eventful sailing trip.

Walter leaned forward, his curiosity piqued, and gestured toward the camera resting on the table. "Could you please show me the images you captured from the depths of the sea?" he inquired.

Responding to his request, Sara gently slid the camera nearer. With deft fingers, she navigated through the series of photographs she had taken during their approach to the village, revealing the mesmerizing underwater garden, the haunting remnants of houses, and the venerable old church. Her fingers paused as she arrived at the image of Minx, eerily suspended in the window of a building. She knew the subsequent images would lead them into the unsettling realm of the ominous field.

"I'm not certain if you'd like to see more." She hesitated, her voice tinged with uncertainty. "The subsequent ones depict the scary field where Minx guided us."

"Yes, please. Show me everything you saw," Walter said.

"We didn't see any other ghosts except the ghost cat," Sara explained, showing the eerie field with the humans as scarecrows and the schools of fish picking at them.

"Oh my, I never thought I'd see that." Walter sighed. "You are an excellent photographer. The images are beautiful even though the last ones are scary."

Granger finished his plate, drank his cider, and turned to Walter. "I believe it's important that we assemble all the surviving residents of our village this evening to confront the apparitions. Every one of them should be present, holding images of their departed loved ones and bearing flowers. Furthermore, we must enlist the services of a priest to join us. If the spirits seek remembrance and long for communal prayer, then it is our solemn duty to provide them with exactly that tonight."

"I'll go and let everyone know what to prepare for tonight," Walter declared as he rose. "We are fortunate to have a new priest among us, and he will undoubtedly know the appropriate words to convey. I will inform everyone to convene here tonight, approximately around ten. Our task is to transform the square into a place of remembrance for our dearly departed." Walter departed in haste, heartened by the glimmer of hope that Granger and Sara had offered him—or perhaps it was akin to absolution of his past sins...

Sara and Granger were left alone in the inn. Sara broke the silence, her words accompanied by a giggle as she savored the food. "The food here is quite tasty," she remarked, her amusement evident. Granger couldn't help but join in her laughter, his own chuckles resonating in the quaint setting. There was no real reason to laugh, except relief from the horrors they saw earlier.

"It truly is," he agreed, a wistful tone creeping into his voice. "The day would have been utterly perfect if it weren't for those eerie scarecrows. The underwater vistas were nothing short of breathtaking."

The entire situation felt surreal, a strange juxtaposition of enjoyment and impending doom. As they indulged in their lunch, an unsettling awareness loomed over them. They knew that the spectral procession would soon arrive to claim their next victim unless they could somehow intervene and put an end to their haunting.

"Do you believe that will work?" Sara asked, referring to the plan they had just suggested to Walter.

"Yes, it should help, but if it doesn't, Walter might have to give up his life. If the ghosts want revenge, he's the one they blame for the village's sinking into the sea," Granger replied.

Chapter 20
The Ghosts return

GRANGER AND SARA WENT to rest in their room while Walter went around the village to inform the villagers of the new plan to please and get rid of the ghosts. Everyone agreed to do what he suggested, and even the priest promised to hold a communal prayer service.

Walter put a new sign on the cobblestone square, renaming it as Memorial Square. He glanced around to make sure that the sign was visible from all directions, and it was.

As the sun dipped below the horizon, casting a warm, golden hue across the village square, the villagers began to gather. The scent of blooming wildflowers and the gentle whisper of leaves in the evening breeze created a hopeful yet anticipating atmosphere. They carried the pictures and flowers they placed around the square and sat on the rustic wooden benches to wait for the communal prayer services to start. Oil lamps and candles were placed around the square to give more light to the service. Usually, the village was pitch black after sunset because everyone feared the ghosts and stayed quietly in the dark, waiting for them to disappear.

The priest brought a stand and placed it in the middle of the square for the service. As the villagers filled the square, they formed a large, diverse congregation, young and old, standing side by side, united in their faith and sense of community.

Walter, Sara, and Granger joined the others as they all waited for the ghosts to appear. The priest, a wise and revered figure, led the service from the middle of the square. His voice, rich with age and wisdom, carried the prayers and chants through the square. The villagers joined in, their voices harmonizing as they sang songs of devotion and gratitude.

As the prayers reached their crescendo, a chilly breeze blew over the square. The flickering candles and lanterns cast strange, dancing shadows on the cobblestones. The singing quieted as the villagers exchanged worried and scared glances, their devotion giving way to unease. One after another, they turned their gaze toward the sea.

A ghostly procession emerged from the water, advancing toward the square. The villagers gasped in fear. The ghosts' translucent forms were illuminated by a soft, ethereal light. Dressed in old-fashioned attire, they moved with a graceful and haunting elegance.

The parade consisted of villagers who had long passed away, their faces bearing expressions of both sorrow and longing. Their footsteps made no sound as they glided across the cobblestones.

The villagers watched in awe, some trembling with emotion, as the ghostly procession continued its silent march. It seemed as though these spirits were participating in the communal prayer service, seeking solace and connection with their living descendants.

As the parade reached the square, the priest lowered his head in a gesture of reverence. The villagers followed suit. It was a moment of profound unity between the living and the departed, a bridge between the past and the present.

Sara and Granger stared at the ghosts, awaiting what they would do next. The ghosts floated around the square, viewing the pictures and flowers and then around the living. Only one ghost, an elderly man, stopped in front of Walter. He pointed at him with his hand.

Walter paled. "Father, I know I was wrong. It was all my fault."

The ghosts stopped and turned their faces to Walter and his father. They all gathered around the two of them, and with a united front, they took Walter with them, continuing their path back to the sea and disappearing from sight, leaving the village square once more, bathing in the soft glow of the candles and oil lamps.

Sara turned to Granger. "Did they take Walter because of what he did in the past?"

Granger nodded. "I think so. He was the human sacrifice they wanted."

The villagers seemed relieved and resumed their prayers. They had reconnected with their ancestors, and the ghosts had left them alone. Perhaps this would be the last time the ghosts visited them.

Sara and Granger stood up from their bench and were about to walk away when Sara saw the ghost cat Minx again. He seemed to wait for them, glancing back and walking a few steps ahead and then again glancing at them as if checking if they would follow him.

"Let's go see what he wants us to witness," Granger said, and he grabbed Sara by the hand and hurried after Minx. He floated fast ahead, leading them up the hill. Then he stopped and turned around. The village lay down below, looking peaceful and quiet. Some villagers still walked on the streets, returning to their homes.

Minx sat by their feet and stared downward at the village.

"What is it, Minx?" Sara asked, and then it happened.

The ground rumbled, and both Sara and Granger quickly ran backward as the village below them sank into the sea, leaving a deep crater behind. The buildings had vanished under the sea, and now the water was filling the area that used to be the village. Granger looked around and saw Minx sitting still at the edge of the crater.

They stared at it, not believing their eyes. The whole village was gone!

"What just happened?" Sara asked, facing Granger.

"Was this also caused by Walter's old business idea, Geomine company?" Granger wondered. "I don't know."

Sara took out her camera and took a few pictures. "What should we do now? We don't have a car or a place to stay tonight?" She let the camera down, and at that moment, Minx jumped into the camera, hiding inside it. Neither Sara nor Granger noticed what he had done.

"Let's start walking to the next village. We'll just have to contact our insurance and tell them that it was destroyed with the landslide here," Granger replied, placing his arm over her shoulder and turning her away from the place that used to be the village.

Chapter 21
The Epilogue

GRANGER AND SARA WALKED to the next village and got a room in a small and quaint motel. They didn't tell anyone what had happened to them because they didn't believe anyone would believe their story. Besides, if the government or law enforcement ever found out about the missing village, they would believe it was just a natural catastrophe that had destroyed it.

The next morning, Sara started viewing her photos on the camera and gasped. Minx's face stared at her through the glass in the back of the camera.

"Granger, come here," she called her husband who came to see what was wrong.

"Look at this," she handed him the camera.

"That's Minx. Is he inside your camera?"

"It looks like he is. I didn't see where he disappeared when we left the site of the village," Sara admitted. "He must have entered inside my camera back then. What should I do with him?"

"I don't know. We can't get him out. He's a ghost. I guess he will come out when he wants to do so," Granger replied.

"I can't view any of my photos because he's staring at me," Sara complained.

"You can still use your camera and take pictures, I hope."

"I don't know what they will turn out to be when he's inside," Sara muttered.

"Let's find a camera shop in this town and get you a replacement one," Granger suggested pulling her in his arms and kissing her. And later that day, Sara got her new camera and from that moment on, she carried two cameras.

The following night, Minx woke them up with an eerie meowing and floating around the motel room his eyes gleaming with otherworldly shine.

"What's wrong, Minx?" Sara asked.

"Perhaps he wants to go back home," Granger suggested placing the pillow over his head, so he didn't have to hear the noise Minx was making. After two hours of shrilling meowing, Minx returned to the camera, and the rest of the night was quiet.

"Should we go back to the village again? I don't want Minx to keep us up every night?" Sara asked the next morning.

"Yes, let's do that," Granger agreed and after breakfast, they went to rent a ship and new snorkeling gear and went sailing.

The day was beautiful. The sun was shining on a clear sky, and the sea was calm.

As the voyage continued and their vessel approached the very spot where the once-thriving village had stood, Granger skillfully brought the engine to a halt. With a practiced hand, Granger released the anchor, its heavy chain unfurling with a gentle splash into the crystalline depths below. Next, they donned their snorkeling gears before lowering themselves into the sea.

The world seemed to hold its breath as if paying homage to the ghostly remnants of the village.

When Sara reached the surface, Minx reappeared and floated away from her camera into the depths of the sea. Sara gestured to Granger, and he nodded. He'd seen Minx too.

They followed him back to the ghost village which was now double the size as before. The newer buildings were not covered with any underwater growth like the older buildings were. The schools of fish swam around and through the windows curious to see what the new part of the village had brought them.

Minx, their enigmatic guide through the shadowy depths of the underwater village, led his human companions with a sense of foreboding purpose back to the very field where they had previously stumbled upon the haunting tableau of human scarecrows. The oppressive silence hung heavy in the air, as though the very land itself held its breath in fearful anticipation.

Arriving at the field, Minx halted, his ethereal slender figure silhouetted against dark water. He turned to face his companions, his eyes aglow with an eerie, phosphorescent light that pierced through the inky darkness, capturing their attention and locking them in a stern gaze and gesturing toward the scary field.

Sara and Granger turned their eyes to the field fearing what they would witness. Then, as though he had made sure his message had been delivered to his companions, Minx melted into the velvety cloak of water, leaving Sara and Granger to witness the new horrors. They didn't see Minx again. They were left with only the haunting memory of his glowing eyes.

In the center of this forsaken field stood a new scarecrow, a grotesque parody of what it once was. It was not the typical guardian of crops but a grim harbinger of terror. The scarecrow's body was crudely constructed from weathered wooden stakes, bound together with fraying ropes. Tattered remnants of clothing clung to his form, billowing like spectral shrouds in the current. But what sent shivers down their spine was that he was a man who they knew: Walter Katz, the innkeeper. His pallid, lifeless face contorted in a permanent expression of agony. His hollow eyes, once brimming with life, were now empty sockets, staring into the abyss of the night. His feet were encrusted with mud as though he had tried to claw away from the Earth in a nightmarish resurrection. The chilling, unnatural stillness of the field was occasionally interrupted by schools of fish swimming by.

In the darkness of the depths, the dead man tied to the pole served as a horrifying sentinel, a grim reminder that in this forsaken village, the boundaries between the living and the dead had blurred into a terrifying reality.

Sara and Granger looked around to see if they would find the other villagers who were buried with the village last night, but they didn't see them. Perhaps, they were under the rubble or still inside the buildings. They didn't want to go wander around to find out. Sara took a few photos, and then they returned to their ship.

They knew that they would forever carry the haunting image of the human scarecrows in their minds as a reminder of the ghostly adventure they had in the village that vanished.

About the author

Meet Arla Jones, a multi-genre author hailing from the picturesque landscapes of Finland, now making waves in the literary world from the tranquil shores of Michigan. With a penchant for exploring diverse genres, the author captivates readers with tales that traverse the realms of mystery, romance, thriller, sci-fi, and fantasy, weaving intricate narratives that transport audiences to worlds both familiar and fantastical. When not penning captivating stories, the author enjoys gardening and painting.

Also by author Arla Jones

The Ackley Family Saga:

Lord Ackley's Choice

A Rose So Red

Court of Kisses

Jaxon Axis -series:

Jaxon Axis and the First Crime

Jaxon Axis and the Ice Age

The Lost Tomb -series:

The Lost Tomb

The Venemous Dunes

The Mummy Returns

The Lost Oasis of Love

Otis Thorne Thriller series:

Fathers and Sons

Black Dust

The Facility

Death Walks in Washington D.C.

The Ashburn -series:

On Death's Door

Finders Keepers

The Cupid and the Elf -series:

Love Trap

Naughty Elf

The Cursed Banshee

The Attack of the Iguana

Find a full list of serial fiction, novels, and my shop: authorarlajones.com
And also https://beacons.ai/arlajonesbooks

Milton Keynes UK
Ingram Content Group UK Ltd.
UKHW022222051124
450708UK00014B/936